Fun with GRAMMAR
Book 3

MOONSTONE

Published in Moonstone
by Rupa Publications India Pvt. Ltd 2023
7/16, Ansari Road, Daryaganj
New Delhi 110002

Sales centres:
Prayagraj Bengaluru Chennai
Hyderabad Jaipur Kathmandu
Kolkata Mumbai

P-ISBN: 978-93-5702-490-7
E-ISBN: 978-93-5702-323-8

First impression 2023

10 9 8 7 6 5 4 3 2 1

Printed in India

CONTENTS

NOUNS

A noun is a word that names a person, place, animal, or thing.

A noun is also called a **naming word.**

Example: <u>Mom</u> baked a <u>cake</u> for <u>Peter</u> on his <u>birthday.</u>

Read the paragraph below and underline all the nouns:

Bob, Paul, Robert, and Martin are playing with a football in a playground. The ground has swings and beautiful flowers all around. Sara is on the slide. Her friend is on the swing. Children are having a lot of fun.

All **nouns** can be classified into two groups of **nouns,** either proper noun or common noun.

A **proper** noun is used to refer to a specific person, place, or object. E.g. **John** is a very smart boy.

Christina lives in **Singapore.**

Proper nouns must begin with capital letters.

A **common** noun is used to refer to a class of people, animals, places or objects. E.g. John is a very smart **boy.**

These are words for people

Doctor

Teacher

Police Man

Sweeper

These are words for animals and birds.

Parrot   **Zebra**   **Wolf**   **Cuckoo**

These are words for place.

School   **Hospital**   **Police Station**   **Museum**

These are words for things.

 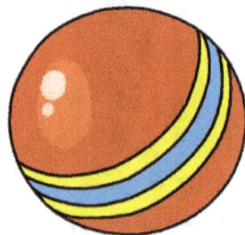  

School bag   **Ball**   **Dice**   **Balloons**

A **Read the following passage. Circle all the proper nouns and underline all the common nouns.**

Last Christmas, my father took us to Bangkok on vacation. We saw a lot of Buddhist temples there. After spending two days there, we went to Koh Samui. Koh Samui is famous for its beaches. We stayed at a resort near Lamai Beach. We had so much fun playing in the sand and waves. We spent a lot of time lying in the sun, too. We met some new friends from Georgia. The entire week was pure joy.

B **Underline the nouns in the sentences below. Write the nouns on the apples below and colour them green if it is a proper noun and red if it is a common noun.**

1. Paul and Ricky are flying kites on the beach.

2. Monday is the first day of the week.

3. Jim Hawkins lives with his mother in Copenhagen.

4. Ted had bought his running shoes from this store.

5. The family went to Disneyland on vacation.

6. Susie loves watching movies on the weekends.

7. Mike takes his dog, Rusty, to the park every day.

8. Kerry gave flowers to Josephine on her birthday.

9. Harry is my best friend.

10. February is the shortest month of the year.

Common nouns can be **countable or uncountable.**

Countable nouns refer to something that can be counted. They have both singular and plural forms.

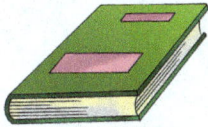   

| **Book** | **Cup** | **Berries** | **Panda** |

Countable nouns (Count nouns) can be preceded by *a; an or a number...*

Some nouns refer to things that cannot be counted, so they are known as uncountable nouns .

| **Milk** | **Butter** | **Sugar** | **Rain** |

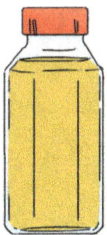   

| **Oil** | **Wood** | **Wine** | **Flour** |

Uncountable nouns are always in the singular; they are not preceded by a number.

ABSTRACT NOUNS

A noun denoting an idea, quality, or state rather than a concrete object is called an **abstract noun**.

Examples: happiness, courage, danger, truth

- The sight of sunrise is **beautiful.**

- Who killed President Kennedy is a real **mystery.**

- Sometimes it takes **courage** to tell the **truth.**

- Their lives were full of **sadness.**

A **Underline all the abstract nouns from the sentences given below. First one is done for you.**

1. Lara had a childhood full of love and happiness.

2. The dove is a symbol of peace.

3. Mark had lot of fun in the water park.

4. I thought bees are attracted to flowers by sight and smell.

5. He takes pride in his job.

6. He cannot control his anger.

7. I had a nightmare last night.

8. Every time I hear the national anthem, my heart fills up with patriotism.

9. My grandfather is full of wisdom.

10. My manager wished me luck for my new project.

B **Fill in the blanks by choosing a suitable abstract noun from the clue box given below.**

> decision   confidence   pleasure   honesty
> education   noise   integrity   happiness   policy

1.   Pam is saving her money for her _____.

2.   _____ means different things to different people.

3.   Megan has the _____ to clear the competitive exam.

4.   The daughter's acceptance of her mother's advice helped her make her _____.

5.   Lot of _____ is coming from across the street..

6.   _____ is the best _____.

7.   My grandfather is a man of _____.

8.   It was a _____ to meet you.

C **Write the correct form of noun in the blanks related to the words in brackets.**

Steve had just moved to Manchester and was looking for an _____ (accommodate). He was a financial consultant with a multinational company. He was given _____ (promote) and his company had organized his transfer to the head office.

He had an _____ (ambitious) to buy a big house with a garden and a swimming pool because he was in a serious _____ (relate) and was thinking of _____ (marry). However, he soon realized that he would not be able to afford to make the regular mortgage _____ (pay) that a house would involve. So he had to settle for a flat.

11

SINGULAR AND PLURAL NOUNS

Singular noun names one person, place, thing, or idea.

Plural noun names more than one person, animal, place, thing, or idea.

Example

Singular	Plural
One cap	Four caps
One dog	Two Dogs

Plural Noun Rules

Most singular nouns are made plural by simply putting an -s at the end. There are many different rules for making nouns plural, depending on what letter a noun ends in.

How to form plural nouns

- **For regular nouns, add 's'.**

Example: cat-cats; friend-friends

- **For nouns ending in -s, -x, -sh, -ch or -ss, add 'es'.**

Example: bus-buses; box- boxes; dish-dishes; church-churches; glass-glasses

- **For nouns ending with consonants followed by -y, change -y to -i and then add 'es'.**

Example: party- parties; city-cities

- **For nouns ending in -f, change -f to -v and then add 'es'.**

Example: thief- thieves; leaf- leaves

- **For nouns ending in -fe, change -fe to -v and then add 'es'.**

Example: knife- knives; life- lives

- **For nouns ending in -o, add 'es'.**

Example: mango- mangoes; tomato- tomatoes

A **Choose a suitable noun from the clue box given below and complete the sentences with their correct form.**

hall	star	computer	cat	person	dish
paper	mango	pond	man	movie	banana

1. We went fishing at the _____ last week.

2. There are a lot of new _____ in the computer lab.

3. There are three _____ waiting for you in front of the school gate.

4. Today we are going to watch a _____ in the evening.

5. Please wash the dirty _____ in the sink.

6. There are many _____ in the sky.

7. Can you please give me a piece of _____.

8. The hall is full of _____.

9.   I saw a _____ walking on the sidewalk.

10.   My sister loves to eat _____ and _____ .

Plural Noun Rules for Irregular Nouns

Some irregular nouns follow no specific rules.

Example:

child – children;   goose – geese;   man – men;   woman – women;
tooth – teeth;   foot – feet;   mouse – mice;   person – people

B **Write plurals for the nouns given below:**

dollar	_____	donkey	_____	couch	_____
key	_____	goose	_____	knife	_____
woman	_____	prefix	_____	pony	_____
bush	_____	wife	_____	glass	_____
person	_____	mouse	_____	beach	_____
fox	_____	tooth	_____	foot	_____

Some words do not change.

Example: *Sheep- sheep; hair- hair; deer- deer*

Some words are plural and have no singular form.

Example: *trousers, scissors, alms, cattle, clothes, pants, pliers*

COLLECTIVE NOUN

A collective noun is the word that is used to represent a group of people, animals, or things.

Examples:

a flock of sheep   a swarm of bees   a bunch of keys

A **Complete the sentences below with the correct collective noun from the word bank.**

1. Our soccer _____ has won the championship title this year.

2. A _____ of musicians are performing on the stage.

3. A _____ of lions circled buffalo.

4. A _____ of ants lived under the log.

5. My father bought my mom a beautiful _____ of flowers.

6. The police are looking for a _____ of robbers.

7. The _____ of birds flew over my head.

8. A _____ of cards is lying in my drawer.

9. _____ of soldiers is called to rescue the boy caught in the flood.

10. A _____ of fish swam past our boat.

> bouquet,   band,   colony,   shoal,   team,
> gang,   army,   flock,   pride,   deck

15

B Complete the crossword below

1. A _____ of bees.

2. A _____ of ants.

3. A _____ of ships.

4. A class of s_____ .

5. A _____ of kittens.

6. A _____ of whales.

7. A _____ of sailors.

8. A clutch of c_____ .

9. A _____ of fish.

10. A choir of s_____ .

11. A _____ of flowers.

12. A _____ of buffalo.

13. A _____ of musicians.

14. A _____ of birds.

15. A _____ of dogs.

MASCULINE AND FEMININE NOUN

Masculine nouns are the words that describe **male** persons (or animals).

Man	Boy	Tiger

Feminine nouns are the words that describe **female** persons (or animals).

Woman	Girl	Tigress

Below are some more examples of masculine and feminine nouns for people:

waiter	waitress
father	mother
bridegroom	bride
witch	wizard
headmaster	headmistress
uncle	aunt
nephew	niece
emperor	empress
brother	sister

Example: stewardess, tigress, hostess, princess

Below are some more examples of masculine and feminine nouns for animals:

cock/ rooster	hen
lion	lioness
bull	cow
fox	vixen
dog	bitch
stallions	mare
colt	filly
ram	ewe
buck	doe
drake	duck

A   Match the masculine gender with the feminine gender.

1. manageress		queen
2. heir		bachelor
3. landlord		grandfather
4. king		widow
5. master		manager
6. actor		mister
7. spinster		heiress
8. grandmother		landlady
9. widower		actress

B   Fill in the following blanks with the correct gender.

1. My _____ is an engineer while my mother is a teacher.

2. The _____ does all the hunting while the lion feeds on the meat first.

3. My nephew stays in New York where as my _____ lives with her mother in Mumbai.

4. Though our landlady is a sweet lady but our _____ is very rude.

5. Whenever the king goes out for hunting, he always takes his _____ along.

C **Underline the nouns in the following sentences and write down their opposite gender in the space given. The first one is done for you.**

1. The two <u>women</u> laughed at her joke.

   ___Men___

2. Nancy is not a spinster because she's still married to her high school sweetheart.

   _____

3. A wicked witch enchanted her, so she could not rule her kingdom.

   _____

4. The Queen waved to the crowd from an open horse-drawn carriage.

   _____

5. All the actors are present here for the award ceremony.

   _____

6. The bride is looking so beautiful in her wedding gown.

   _____

7. The coffee that the flight steward served was cold.

   _____

8. The horse stumbled, and his rider was thrown heavily to the ground.

   _____

COMMON GENDER

Nouns that can be referred to as either **male** or **female** are said to be **common gender nouns.**

Children

Teacher

Artist

A **Classify the following nouns according to their gender and write them in the appropriate flower petals.**

rooster   peahen

friend   drake

bitch   bull-elephant

rams   neighbour

doe   baby

police-officer   emperor

vixen   stallion

judge   wife

doctor   goose

friend   gentleman

parent   niece

aunt   husband

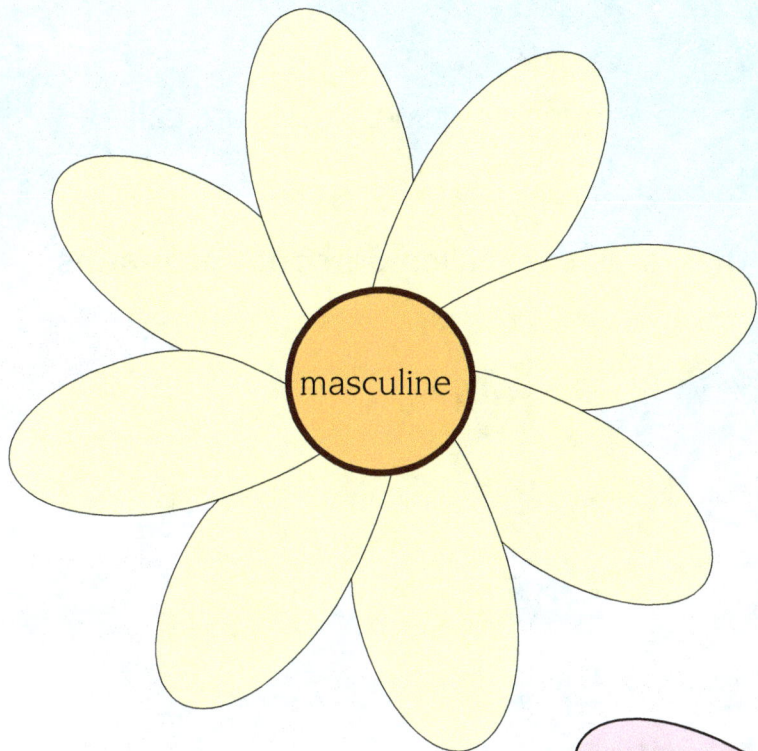

masculine

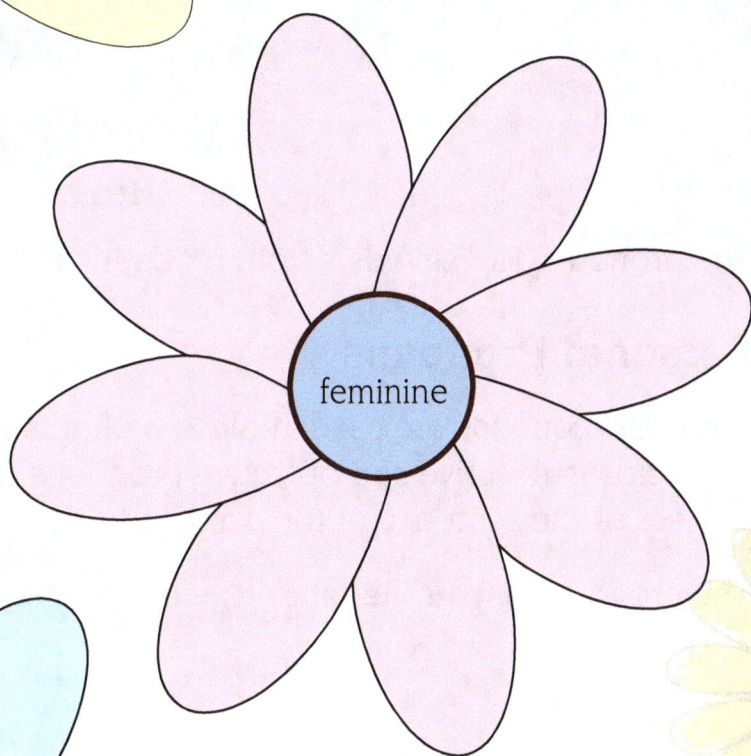

feminine

common

PRONOUNS

Words that are used in place of common nouns or proper nouns are called **pronouns.**

The words **he, she , I , you, we, they,** and **it** are called **personal pronouns.**

He is Mark. **He** is my friend.

The pronoun "He" saved us from repeating the name Mark again.

Personal Pronouns

Personal pronouns are used in place of a person's name. They consist of two kinds: subjective and objective pronouns. That is, they either act as the subject of the sentence or the object of the sentence.

The pronouns **I, you, he, she, it, we,** and **they** are the subject of the sentence.

For Example:

- **I** am Liza. Show a girl speaking 'I am Liza' in a bubble.

- **You** are Maria.

- **She** is my sister.

- **He** is my brother.

- **They** went to the store, etc.

Subject pronouns are those pronouns that perform the action in a sentence.

The pronouns *me*, *you*, *us*, *them*, *him*, *her*, and *it* are the object of the sentence.

For Example:

- Give this bag to **me.**

- Look at **her.**

- I want to sit beside **you.**

- Mary put the gift under **it.**

> An object is the person, animal or thing which receives the action of the verb.

A **Find the pronouns in the sentences below. Highlight them with a coloured pencil. The first one is done for you.**

1. Mark was disturbing the class, so he was asked to sit quietly.

2. I went to the park.

3. The baby is crying. He is hurt.

4. John had a cap. It is red in colour.

5. Nancy has a doll. It has beautiful blue eyes.

6. Peter is a kind boy. He always helps others.

7. The cows have finished grazing. They are resting under the tree.

8. Mrs. Smith teaches at a school. She is a teacher.

9. Hannah loves to play guitar. She is a rockstar.

10. We are going to watch a movie today.

B **Complete the following sentences by writing the appropriate pronouns.**

1. Baby birds cannot fly. The mother bird has to feed ____them____.

2. I have a dog. _____ is called Lucky.

3. This is my friend Betty. _____ ate all the cupcakes on the plate.

4. Mr. Taylor is my father. _____ is a lawyer.

5. Mac loves riding my bicycle. I sometimes lend _____ to _____.

6. I am looking for Katie. Has anyone seen _____ ?

7. Pick up your toys and put _____ away.

8. Find George and tell _____ dinner is ready.

9. Passengers are reminded to carry _____ hand luggage with them.

10. Jane and Betty! _____ may go out to play now.

Fill in each blank with a suitable pronoun.

Today is Sara's birthday. Her father has bought a beautiful cake for _____.

The cake has nine candles on _____. Sara is so excited to see _____.

Sara's mother sews a beautiful dress for _____ Sara likes it very much too.

Here comes Sara's friends. _____ has invited _____ to her

birthday party. _____ have brought presents for _____ . She puts

_____ on the table near her birthday cake. Sara thanks everyone for

coming to her birthday party.

COMPOUND WORDS

Compound words are formed when two or more **words** are put together to form a new **word** with a new meaning.

 +

Butter   **fly**   **Butterfly**

A **Look at the pictures, guess the words and write the new word in the space provided.**

 +    _____

 +    _____

 + 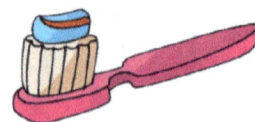   _____

28

 +  _____

 +  _____

 + 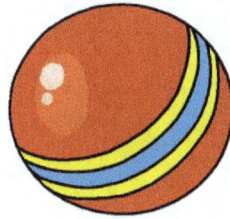 _____

 +  _____

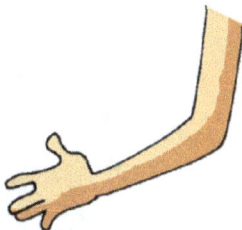 +  _____

29

B Join the words given below to the words from the clue box to make a compound word. Use the pictures as clues.

Man   Bin   Paper   Watch   Robe   Berry

Dust   _____   =   _____

Snow + _____   =   _____

Straw + _____   =   _____

Wrist + _____   =   _____

News + _____   =   _____

Bath + _____   =   _____

ADJECTIVE

An **adjective** is a **describing word.** Adjectives are the **words that are used to describe people, place, or things.** The Adjective usually comes **before** the noun it describes, but sometimes it can come **after** the noun, later in the sentence.

Peter is wearing a blue shirt and white shorts.

Ted's father is a tall man.

A **Write a word to describe each of these nouns. One has been done for you.**

Noun	Describing Word
Hair	Long
Grandfather	_____
Grass	_____

Crow   _____   

Elephant   _____   

Duck   _____   

Storybook   _____   

Rope   _____   

Ice Cream   _____   

Rose   _____   

1. A tall colouring book is lying on the table.

2. This is a long rope.

3. The elephant has a long trunk.

4. Steve is writing with a red pencil.

5. An empty basket is lying on the kitchen table.

6. We live in a big house.

C **Complete the sentences given below with an appropriate adjective from the clue box.**

few	brave	windy	small	grey	loud
chocolate		some	long	expensive	

1. I love _____ cake.

2. A giraffe has a _____ neck.

3. The _____ puppy is running all over the place.

4. The _____ boy saves his friend from drowning.

5. My grandmother has _____ hair.

6. There are a _____ eggs in the basket.

7. This is an _____ dress.

8. May I have _____ coffee, please?

9. Baby got scared to hear the _____ thunder.

10. Chicago is also called a _____ city.

POSSESSIVE ADJECTIVES

A **possessive adjective** shows who **owns** or **possesses** something. The **possessive adjectives** are **my, your, his, her, its, our, their,** and **whose.**

A **Look at the pictures carefully. Then underline the correct adjectives in the brackets.**

1. I am reading (my, its) book.

2. Nancy is combing (their, her) hair.

3. (Their, Its) fur is soft.

4. They are washing (her, their) hands.

VERBS

A **verb** is a word that represents an action or a state of being.

eat	swim	run	sleep

The words, **eat, swim, run,** and **sleep** represents action.

I am tall	Children **are** playing.	Elizabeth **is** a teacher.

Am, are, is are the verbs that tell us about the **state of subjects** (I, children, Elizabeth). These verbs connect a subject with a word that describes or identifies.

is, am, are, was, were are **verbs - to - be** or are also called the **linking verbs.**

A Fill in the blanks with is, am, are, was or were.

1. Sally _____ swimming in the pool.

2. The doctor _____ here just now.

3. I _____ an engineer.

4. The students _____ in the classroom now.

5. You _____ late yesterday.

6. Mr. Mathew _____ always helpful.

7. Maddy and Bob _____ absent yesterday.

8. Paul and Jill _____ our neighbours.

9. I _____ thin.

10. Yesterday _____ Thursday.

B Fill in the blanks with the linking verbs.

Sara and Paul _____ at home today. It is their holiday. Paul _____ older than Sara. Last year he _____ in grade 3. This year Sara _____ in grade.

Paul helps her with her studies. They both _____ in St. Anthony's school earlier. Now they _____ in St. Marks. St. Marks _____ near to their home.

SIMPLE PRESENT TENSE

The **present tense** tells us that something is true at the present time, or the action is happening now.

I	Am	
She He Amy	Is	seven years old.
They We You The boys	Are	in Primary 2A

She **is** Miss Becker.

She teaches us Mathematics.

My father is a doctor.

He works in the children's hospital.

Jane and Maria are friends.

They play together.

A **Fill in the blanks with the appropriate verbs in the present tense.**

1. The plane .... at 6.30. (arrive)

2. I will phone you when he .... back. (come)

3. Unless we .... now, we can't be there on time. (start)

4. The sun .... in the east. (rise)

5. The next term .... on Monday. (begin)

6. She .... an engineer. (be)

7. They .... our relatives. (be)

8. When does the train ....? (depart)

9. Let's wait till he .... his work. (finish)

10. Please ring me up as soon as he .... (arrive)

SIMPLE PAST TENSE

The **past tense** tells us that the action has taken place before the present.

I She He Amy	Was	six years old last year.
They We You The boys	Were	in primary 1A last year.

He was happy yesterday.

His mother gave him a present.

My parents were angry at me.

I broke the vase.

A Underline the correct answers. The first one is done for you.

1. Mark and his sister (was/ <u>were</u>) at their cousin's house yesterday.

2. A stranger (was / were) outside my house yesterday.

3. The windows of the car (was/ were) all broken, and the front end was smashed back to the windshield.

4. It (was/ were) getting dark.

5. A bunch of people (was/ were) waiting outside the president's house.

6. You (was/ were) playing outside with your friends when she came.

7. They (was/ were) working together on an important assignment.

8. Steve (was/ were) reluctant to go to hostel.

9. I (was/ were) listening to the music when the doorbell rang.

10. The children (was/ were) very hungry. The mother (was / were) cooking fish for them.

B Fill in the blanks with the simple past tense of the verb in the brackets.

1. Long ago, there _____ (be) a good prince.

2. The prince _____ (love) a kind princess.

3. He _____ (save) the princess from a terrible dragon.

4. He _____ (kill) the dragon with his sword.

5. The princess _____ (marry) the prince.

6. They _____ (live) happily ever after.

7. Peggy _____ (cycle) to school last Monday.

8. The children _____ (buy) presents for their teachers on Teacher's Day.

9. The baby _____ (fall) and hit her head.

10.   A thief _____ (steal) my necklace and bracelet yesterday.

FUTURE TENSE

The **future tense** expresses an action that has not yet happened or a state that does not yet exist.

I **will jump** into the lake.

We **shall go** to the zoo on Sunday.

You **will see** sand dunes in the desert.

We can use shall or will with I and we.
We use will with you, he, she, it and they.

I think I am going to be sick.

A **Complete each sentence by changing the verb in () to future tense.**

1. He (paint) _____ the house.

2. She (study) _____ hard for the examination.

3. I (ask) _____ her to come tomorrow.

4. Tomorrow it (rain) _____.

5. We (serve) _____ lunch at 12: 30.

6. I promise I (make) _____ the bed.

7. Those apples look delicious. I (buy) _____ some.

8. I hope it (not/ rain) _____ on Sunday.

9. The police (catch) _____ the thieves.

10. Every student (have) _____ a laptop next year.

B **Tick the sentences that show a future action.**

1.   A) She is going to school next year.   (√)

     B) I am going to school now.   (   )

45

2.   A) My wife is going to the hospital to have a baby.   ( )

      B) I am going to take care of the baby when it is born.   ( )

3.   A) The horseman is going through the forest.   ( )

      B) He is going to warn Robin Hood that the soldiers are coming. ( )

4.   A) Mr. Jiang is going into the water.   ( )

      B) He is going to swim across the bay.   ( )

5.   A) Tom is going to dine with his girlfriend.   ( )

      B) He is going out of the house now.   ( )

C Change these sentences to past tense.

1. Mother cooks dinner.

_____

2. We run fast.

_____

3. She has a smartphone.

_____

4. The book is in the bag.

_____

5. Andy writes with a pencil.

_____

6. We watch T.V. in the evening.

_____

D **Change these sentences to present tense.**

1. The children sang sweetly.

_____

2. Karan and Steve played in the park.

_____

3. They stood up at once.

_____

4. Shaun drove very fast.

_____

5. Anna wrote neatly.

_____

6. She wore a red coat.

_____

E **Rewrite the sentences below using shall or will.**

1. We wake up at 5 a.m.

_____

2. I put the kettle on.

_____

3. Jane makes the coffee.

_____

4. Sam cuts the bread.

    _____

5. Sue sees to the bags.

    _____

6. Sam and sue book a taxi.

    _____

7. We then look out for a taxi.

    _____

8. When it comes, we load the bags.

    _____

9. I close and lock the door.

    _____

10. Then we are off.

    _____

PREPOSITION

A **preposition** is a **word** or a **set of words** that are used to connect the **position or place** of a **person, place, animal, or thing, to other words within the sentence**.

Peter sat on the chair.	She is hiding under the table.	There is a garden in front of the house.

A Pick out the prepositions in the sentences. Write them on the lines provided.

49

1. There is a tree in the garden. _____

2. There is a nest on the tree branch. _____

3. A baby bird is in the nest. _____

4. Ronny, the dog, is under the tree. _____

5. The mother bird is flying over the nest. _____

6. Roy is running to Ronny. _____

B **Fill in the blanks by choosing the correct preposition from the clue box. First one is done for you.**

at	in	on
across	over	into

1. My little sister was born __on__ 10th October.

2. The eggs are _____ the nest.

3. There is a market _____ the road.

4. Sprinkle some water _____ the flowers.

5. There is a bridge _____ the river.

6. Dinner will be served _____ 7 o' clock.

C Choose the most suitable answer from the options below and complete the sentence.

1. Who are you waiting __for__?

  (a) for   (b) to   (c) from   (d) at

2. We climbed _____ the stairs to go to the top floor.

  a) down   (b) by   (c) up   (d) against

3. Why is Ben hiding _____ the bed?

  a) on   (b) under   (c) up   (d) in

4. Jenny has gone to New Zealand _____ her parents.

  a) along   (b) for   (c) from   (d) with

5. My mother prefers coffee _____ tea.

  a) besides   (b) to   (c) over   (d) on

6. She burst _____ tears.

  a) in   (b) into   (c) with   (d) at

7. Mr. Travis set up a stall _____ the Green Road.

  (a) about   (b) along   (c) through   (d) over

8. Rex is standing _____ Alex and Sam.

  (a) beside   (b) with   (c) between   (d) from

9. I am waiting _____ the bus to come.

  (a) at   (b) for   (c) through   (d) to

10.   Will Ben's training finish _____ evening?

  (a) at   (b) by   (c) on   (d) over

51

CONJUNCTIONS

Conjunctions are words that are used to join words together in a sentence. They are also called as Linking words.

The most common **conjunctions** are **and, but, or** and **because**.

He is in bed because he is sick.	Mother bought some apples and pears.

Mark is small but strong.	Is this a sheep or a goat?

Choose a conjunction from the Word bank: *and, or, but,* and, *because* to join each set of sentences below. The first one is done for you.

1. John is rushing to school <u>because</u> he is late.

2. Passersby looked at his feet _____ laughed.

3. John looked down at his feet _____ he did not laugh.

4. He was confused whether to go on _____ to go back home.

5. People were laughing as he was wearing a green sock _____ a blue one!

> We can use **as, since,** or **for** to replace **because** without changing the meaning of the sentence.

The baby cried **because** he was hungry.

The baby cried **as** he was hungry.

The baby cried **since** he was hungry.

The baby cried **for** he was hungry.

Although and **though** are used to show that something is done when it should not be or cannot be done.

He completed the work, **although** he was very tired.

Though he was very tired, he completed the work.

B **Fill in the blanks with the correct conjunctions from the word box.**

because	and	so	although
while	but	as	though

1. No one believed the shepherd boy,_____ he finally spoke the truth.

2. The crow dropped its meat _____ it opened its mouth to caw.

3. The hare was too sure of itself, _____ it lost the race with the tortoise.

4. The crow dropped pebbles into the pitcher, _____ the water rose to the top.

HOMONYMS

Words having the same spelling and sound but different meanings are called **homonyms.**

Show me your **left** hand.

Some cookies were **left** in the jar.

There is a **park** near my house.

Park the car at the car parking area.

A **Each word in the box has two meanings. Use them to fill in the blanks.**

Bill   match   pen   stick   sink

1. The old lady walks with the _____ .

2. Father paid the _____ at the restaurant.

3. India won the cricket _____ .

4. I need a Fevistick to _____ these pictures.

5. We need a _____ to light a fire.

6. The boat will _____ if the waves wash over it.

7. Small children don't write with a _____ .

8. Put the dirty plates in the _____ .

9. Hen lives in _____ .

10. A kingfisher has a long, sharp, pointed _____ .

COMPREHENSION - A

Read the given passage and answer the questions given below.

Jake is going on a trip. He and Mom take a taxi to the airport. "It's my first plane trip," he tells the taxi driver. "That's great!" the taxi driver says. Jake rolls his suitcase onto the plane. "It's my first plane trip," he tells the pilot. "Welcome aboard," the pilot says. Jake finds his seat and buckles his seatbelt. The plane's engines rumble and roar. Jake opens his backpack and pulls out Panda. "It's my first plane trip," he whispers. He holds Panda's paw. The plane moves faster and faster. Then—Whoosh! On the ground, cars, and houses look like toys. Jake smiles. "Guess what, Panda?" he says. "Flying is fun!"

Answer the following questions:

1. How do Jake and his mom travel to the airport?

     a. in a plane   b. in their car   c. in a taxi   d. in a bus

2. What does the pilot say to Jake?

_____

3. Who is Panda?

a. Jake's brother   b. a large animal   c. Jake's pet   d. a stuffed animal

4. What does Jake whisper to Panda?

_____

5. On the ground, the cars and houses look like toys.

What does the above sentence mean?

a. The cars and houses looked very big.

b. The cars and houses looked very small.

c. The cars and houses did not move.

d. Jake could not see the cars and houses.

COMPREHENSION - B

Read the given passage and answer the questions given below.

The kangaroo is found in Australia. It is nearly as tall as a man. Its front legs are very short. It uses them to hold things. It also uses them to carry food to its mouth. The kangaroo's tail is long, thick, and strong. Its head is like that of a deer. The mother kangaroo has a pocket in its belly; this is where it carries its baby. Kangaroos like to eat grass and leaves. They do not eat meat.

1. Where are the kangaroos found?

_____

2. How does a kangaroo use its front legs?

_____

3. What do kangaroos like to eat?

_____

59

ANSWER KEY

Noun

(A)

Proper Noun

Christmas, Bangkok, Buddhist, koh samui, Lamai Beach, Georgia

Common Noun

Father, Vacation, Temples, Days, Beaches, Resort, Sand, Waves, Sun, Friends, Week

(B)

1. Paul Ricky Beach
2. Monday Day Week
3. Jim Hawkins Mother Copenhagen
4. Ted Shoes Store
5. Family Disneyland Vacation.
6. Susie Movies Weekends
7. Mike Dog Rusty Park Day
8. Kerry Flowers Josephine Birthday
9. Harry Friend
10. Febraury Month Year

Abstract Nouns

(A)

1. chilhood, love and happiness
2. peace
3. fun
4. sight and smell
5. pride
6. anger
7. nightmare
8. patriotism
9. wisdom
10. luck

(B)

1. Education
2. Happiness
3. Confidence
4. decision
5. noise
6. honesty **and** policy
7. integrity
8. pleasure

(C)

accommodation
promotion
ambition
relationship
marriage
payments

Singular and Plural Nouns

(A)

1. Pond
2. Computers
3. Men
4. Movie
5. Dishes
6. Stars
7. Paper
8. People
9. Cat
10. Mangoes, Bananas

(B)

1. dollar - dollars
2. donkey - donkeys
3. couch - couches
4. key - keys
5. goose - geese
6. knife - knives
7. woman - women
8. prefix - prefixes
9. pony - ponies
10. bush - bushes
11. wife - wives
12. glass - glasses
13. person - people
14. mouse - mice
15. beach - beaches
16. fox - foxes
17. tooth - teeth
18. foot - feet

Collective Noun

(A)

1. team
2. band

3. pride
4. colony
5. bouquet
6. gang
7. flocks
8. deck
9. army
10. shoal

(B)

1. swarm
2. colony
3. fleet
4. students
5. litter
6. pod
7. crew
8. chick
9. school
10. singers
11. bouquet
12. herd
13. band
14. flock
15. pack

Masculine And Feminine Noun

(A)

1. Manageress - Manager
2. Heir - Heiress
3. Landlord - Landlady
4. King - Queen
5. Master - Mistress
6. Actor - Actress
7. Spinster - Bachelor
8. Grandmother - Grandfather
9. Widower - Widow

(B)

1. Father
2. Lioness
3. Niece
4. Landlord
5. Queen

(C)

1. Men
2. Bachelor
3. Wizard
4. King
5. Actresses
6. Bridegroom
7. Stewardess
8. Mare

Common Gender

(A)

Masculine:
Rooster, Rams, Stallion, Drake, Bull elephant, Emperor, Husband
Feminine:
Peahen, Vixen, Doe, Goose, Aunt, Bitch, Wife, Niece
Common/ Neuter :
Neighbour, Friend, Baby, Judge, Parent, Police officer, Doctor

Pronoun

(A)

1. He
2. I
3. He
4. It
5. It
6. He
7. They
8. She
9. She
10. We

(B)

1. them
2. it
3. she
4. he
5. it and him
6. her
7. them
8. him

9. thier

10. you

(C)

Today is Sara's birthday. Her father has bought a beautiful cake for <u>her.</u> The cake has nine candles on <u>it.</u> Sara is so excited to see <u>it.</u>

Sara's mother sew a beautiful dress for <u>her.</u> Sara likes it very much too.

Here comes Sara's friends. <u>She</u> has invited <u>them</u> to her birthday party. <u>They</u> have brought presents for <u>her.</u> She puts <u>them</u> on the table near her birthday cake. Sara thanks every one for coming to her birthday party.

Compound Words

(A)

1. Sunflower
2. Rainbow
3. Toothbrush
4. Raincoat
5. Fireman
6. Basketball
7. Cupboard
8. Armchair

(B)

1. bin
2. man
3. berry
4. watch
5. paper
6. robe

Adjective

(A)

1. long
2. old
3. green
4. black
5. big
6. white
7. thick
8. long

9. cold
10. red

(B)

1. tall
2. long
3. long
4. red
5. empty
6. big

(C)

1. Chocolate
2. long
3. small
4. brave
5. grey
6. few
7. expensive
8. some
9. loud
10. windy

Possessive Adjectives

(A)

1. I am reading my book.
2. Nancy is combing her hair.
3. Its fur is soft.
4. They are washing their hands.

Verb

(A)

1. is
2. was
3. am
4. are
5. were
6. is
7. were
8. are
9. am
10. was

(B)

Sara and Paul <u>are</u> at home today. It is their holiday

today. Paul <u>is</u> older than Sara. Last year he <u>was</u> in grade 3. This year Sara <u>is</u> in grade 2. Paul helps her with her studies. They both <u>were</u> in St. Anthony's school earlier. Now they <u>are</u> in St. Marks. St. Marks <u>is</u> near to their home.

Simple Present Tense

(A)

1. The plane arrives at 6.30.
2. I will phone you when he comes back.
3. Unless we start now, we can't be there on time.
4. The sun rises in the east.
5. The next term begins on Monday.
6. She is an engineer.
7. They are our relatives.
8. When does the train depart?
9. Let's wait till he finishes his work.
10. Please ring me up as soon as he arrives.

Simple Past Tense

(A)

1. were
2. was
3. were
4. was
5. were
6. were
7. were
8. was
9. was
10. were and was

(B)

1. was
2. loved
3. saved
4. killed
5. married
6. lived
7. cycled
8. bought
9. fell
10. stole

Future Tense

(A)

1. He will paint the house.
2. She will study hard for the examination.
3. I shall ask her to come tomorrow.
4. Tomorrow it will rain.
5. We shall serve lunch at 12:30.
6. I promise I will make the bed.
7. Those apples look delicious. I shall buy some.
8. I hope it will not rain on Sunday.
9. The police will catch the thieves.
10. Every student will have a laptop next year.

(B)

1. A
2. B
3. B
4. B
5. A

(C)

1. Mother cooked dinner.
2. We ran fast.
3. She had a smartphone.
4. The book was in the bag.
5. Andy wrote with a pencil.
6. We watched T.V. in the evening.

(D)

1. The children sing sweetly.
2. Karan and Steve play in the park.
3. They stand up at once.
4. Shaun drives very fast.
5. Anna writes neatly.
6. She wears a red coat.

(E)

1. We shall wake up at 5 a.m.
2. I will put the kettle on.
3. Jane will make the coffee.
4. Sam will cut the bread.
5. Sue will see to the bags.
6. Sam and Sue will book a taxi.
7. We shall then look out for a taxi.
8. When it comes, we will load the bags.

9. I shall close and lock the door.
10. Then we will be off.

Preposition

(A)

1. in
2. on
3. in
4. under
5. over
6. to

(B)

1. on
2. in
3. across
4. on
5. over
6. at

(C)

1. for
2. up
3. under
4. with
5. over
6. into
7. along
8. between
9. for
10. by

Conjunctions

(A)

1. because
2. and
3. but
4. or
5. and

(B)

1. although
2. as
3. but
4. so

Homonyms

(A)

1. stick
2. bill
3. match
4. stick
5. match
6. sink
7. pen
8. sink
9. pen
10. bill

Comprehension - A

1. in a taxi
2. "Welcome aboard."
3. a stuffed animal
4. "It's my first plane trip."
5. The cars and houses looked very small.

Comprehension - B

1. Kangaroos are found in Australia.
2. Kangaroos use their front legs to hold things and carry food to their mouth.
3. Kangaroos like to eat grass and leaves; they do not eat meat.